George Darley

Nepenthe

A Poem in Two Cantos

George Darley

Nepenthe
A Poem in Two Cantos

ISBN/EAN: 9783744769648

Printed in Europe, USA, Canada, Australia, Japan

Cover: Foto ©Andreas Hilbeck / pixelio.de

More available books at **www.hansebooks.com**

NEPENTHE

A Poem in Two Cantos

BY

GEORGE DARLEY

WITH AN INTRODUCTION BY

R. A. STREATFEILD

LONDON
ELKIN MATHEWS, VIGO STREET
MDCCCXCVII

INTRODUCTION

GEORGE DARLEY never was a popular poet, even during his lifetime, and perhaps, after half a century of neglect, it is now too late to rekindle the dying embers of his fame. His poetry is unquestionably not of the type which commands general appreciation, but he surely deserves to stand among the " poets' poets," by the side of his friend Beddoes, whose genius he was one of the first to recognise.

Darley published but little during his lifetime, and that little is now rarely to be met with, but within the last few years there have been two valuable reprints of some of his least accessible works. In 1890 Canon Livingstone, a kinsman of the poet, published a slender collection of Darley's lyrical poems for private circulation, and two years later his pastoral play, " Sylvia; or, The May Queen," was reprinted under the careful editorship of Mr. J. H. Ingram.

But Darley's lyrical poems, though their diction is often exquisitely felicitous, are little calculated to give a proper idea of his remarkable imaginative power, and " Sylvia," graceful as much of it is, is very far from being his most characteristic work. If he is ever to win the recognition to which such critics as Coleridge have thought him entitled, his passport to the glories of post-humous fame must be " Nepenthe," a poem which, though occasionally marred by wilful eccentricity, exhibits the scope of his poetical faculty in a more striking light than any of his other works.

Darley's history has been told before, but it may be well to recapitulate its leading incidents. He was born in Ireland in 1795, and was educated at Dublin. For what profession he was originally intended is not known, but a serious and apparently incurable habit of stammering with which he was afflicted, appeared to present an insurmountable barrier to success in any of the learned professions, and he therefore determined to devote himself to a literary career. He migrated to London, and produced his first poem, "The Errors of Ecstasie," in 1822. Soon afterwards he joined the staff of the "London Magazine," to which he contributed both prose and verse. In 1826 came "The Labours of Idleness," a collection of prose tales and essays, which was reprinted a few years later, with some additional matter, as "The New Sketch-Book." In 1827 appeared his pastoral play, "Sylvia; or, The May Queen;" in 1839, "Nepenthe;" and in 1840 and 1841, two historical plays, "Thomas A'Becket," and "Ethelstan." Darley died in 1846. His career throughout was a disappointment The unlucky impediment in his speech debarred him from intercourse with any but intimate friends, and as time went on, and his habits became more and more those of a recluse, he became estranged from many of these also. In Mr. Edmund Gosse's recently-published edition of the letters of Beddoes there is a striking vignette of Darley as he appeared in 1824. "Darley is a tallish, slender, pale, light-eyebrowed, gentle-looking bald-pate, in a brown sourtout [*sic*], with a duodecimo under his arm—stammering to a most provoking degree, so much so as to be almost inconversible." Beddoes and Darley were never intimate, though they seem to have met pretty often about this time, but Beddoes entertained a certain respect for Darley's poetry, and even speaks of him as the man upon whom the mantle of Shelley might conceivably have fallen. In Darley's "Labours of Idleness" there are not infrequent references to himself and his career, some of which seem to be worth quoting. I do not know that they have been noticed by any previous biographer. The book appeared under the pseudonym of Guy Penseval, prefaced by a rather elaborate piece of mystification, which purports to explain how the supposed editor came by the various tales included in the work. In it occurs this passage : " Of the four remaining articles, this is a straight-forward account. The last is written by an obscure young man, one G—— D——, who twinkled in the literary hemisphere a year or two ago, but has lately disappeared. He was rather an anomaly. Some of his friends were good enough to call him a genius, for which he always (being of a very grateful temper) made them a bow. Others of them thought he was mad, and were even considerate enough to inform him of his deplorable situation; to these also he returned every due acknowledgment. I myself, who ought to have known him, could not say exactly which he was. Sometimes I thought him the one, sometimes the other, sometimes neither, sometimes both. Yet we had been inseparable for thirty years ! I loved him as myself; but he, wayward mortal ! though by inclination I am sure my sincerest well-wisher, oftentimes exhibited himself my greatest enemy. He has frequently, on pretence of doing me a service, injured me beyond reparation; and indeed to him are almost all the misfortunes of my life attributable. But I could never prevail on myself to throw him off, although by a most unhandsome trick of his (spirting vinegar through his teeth or out of a quill) he mortally offended several of my best friends, who would never afterwards approach me, but always took off their hats at a respectful distance. Notwithstanding this foolish propensity, he was naturally of an hypochondriac, melancholy disposition, which was no doubt augmented by the nervous sensibility of his frame, and the delicacy of his constitution. Such a temperament is usually coupled with an imaginative brain, and a romantic turn of thinking; he was indeed a day-dreamer of no ordinary extravagance, and was perpetually creating such labyrinths of thought around him, that no wonder if he was sometimes lost in them. But in the main he was as sound as I am, and could even laugh as I did at the excesses into which his enthusiasm led him. Some of his compositions were less irregular, and indeed as works of fancy their novelty of conception and imagery may perhaps recommend them with those who have just as severe a contempt for meteors and just as profound an admiration for paving-stones, as I wish them."

The first tale in the book, "The Enchanted Lyre," is written in the first person, the hero being a philosophic youth, dwelling in a romantic retreat upon the banks of a waterfall. Much of it is evidently autobiographical ; indeed, Darley's sketch of his own character corresponds pretty closely to the description left us by his friends.

"Solitude is not so much my necessity as my inclination. I have neither love for society, nor those agreeable qualities of mind, manner, and disposition, which would make society love me. To confess a truth, I once made the experiment, more from curiosity than a desire to succeed: but it was like to have cost me my own good opinion, as well as that of my acquaintances, who, whilst I remained in seclusion, voted me a philosopher, but the moment I exhibited myself in society, set me down as a fool. I always found myself so embarrassed in the presence of others, and everyone so embarrassed in mine,—I was so perpetually infringing the rules of politeness, saying or doing awkward things, telling unpalatable truths, or giving heterodox opinions on matters long since established as proper, agreeable, becoming, and the contrary, by the common creed of the world; there was so much to offend, and so little to conciliate in my manners; arrogant at one time, puling at another; dull, when I should have been entertaining; loquacious when I should have been silent—for I could sometimes be very witty out of place, and very instructive upon uninteresting topics. I was, in fine, such an incomprehensible, unsystematized, impersonal compound of opposite qualities, with no overwhelming power of mind to carry off, as I have seen in others, these heterogeneous particles in a flood of intellectuality, that I quickly perceived obscurity was the sphere in which Nature had destined me to shine; and that the very best compliment my friends could pay me, when I had left them, was to forget me and my faults for ever. At first, indeed, there were several persons who liked, or seemed to like, me from a certain novelty or freshness in my manner ; but as soon as that wore off, they liked me no longer.   I was an 'odd being,' or a 'young man of genius, but very singular ;' something to fill up the gap of tea-table conversation, when the fineness of the evening and the beauty of the prospect had been already discussed by the party."

If we are to believe the records of his contemporaries, the ill-concealed bitterness of this diatribe represents the normal tone of Darley's sentiment towards the world at large.   Miss Mitford says bluntly that he withdrew from society in disgust at his failure to win the popular ear, but it is more charitable to suppose that the impediment in his speech, the "mask upon his mind," as Darley himself called it, was at least as much responsible for the misanthropic seclusion in which his later years were passed as the cold reception of his poems.

"Nepenthe" was privately printed in or about the year 1839.   Darley's friends were few in number, and the impression was probably a very small one.   The poem seems to have passed almost unnoticed, and it is rarely

mentioned, even in the literary memoirs of
the period.   Nowadays it is *rarissime*, indeed
the British Museum copy, from which this
reprint has been made, is probably unique.
Nothing was too small or insignificant for
the wide circle of Miss Mitford's literary
sympathies, and in her " Recolleĉtions " she
discourses about " Nepenthe " with delight-
ful garrulity.

" It is," she says, " as different in appearance
from the common run of books printed for
private distribution, which are usually models
of typography, of paper, and of binding, as it
is in subjeĉt and composition.   Never was
so thorough an abnegation of all literary
coxcombry as was exhibited in the outward
form of " Nepenthe," unless there may be
some suspicion of affeĉtation in the remarkable homeliness, not to say squalor, of the
strange little pamphlet, as compared with
the grace and refinement of the poetry.
Printed with the most imperfeĉt and broken
types, upon a coarse, discoloured paper, like
that in which a country shopkeeper puts up
his tea, with two dusky leaves of a still

dingier hue, at least a size too small, for cover, and garnished at top and bottom with a running margin in his own writing, such (resembling nothing but a street ballad or an old ' broadside ') is the singular disguise of this striking poem.   There is no reading the whole, for there is an intoxication about it that turns one's brain.   Such a poet could never have been popular.   But he was a poet."

" Nepenthe " from the first was misunderstood. Miss Mitford, although she was polite enough to tell Darley that she preferred it to " Sylvia," seems never to have got to the end of it.   Even so good a Darleian as Mr. Ingram, the latter-day editor of " Sylvia," dismisses it as a bizarre production.   It is not without occasional eccentricities, and much of the second Canto is exceedingly obscure, but it would be difficult to name a poem published between the death of Byron in 1824 and what Matthew Arnold calls the decisive appearance of Tennyson in 1842— a period of admitted poetical aridity—more conspicuous for sustained imaginative power and magnificent sonority of diction.   Darley

has occasional obligations to Keats, but on
the other hand the careful reader will find
in "Nepenthe" not a few passages which
curiously anticipate familiar lines in our later
poets.

Miss Mitford's annotated copy of "Nepenthe" seems unfortunately to have disappeared, but a letter is extant from Darley
to his friend H. F. Chorley, giving a brief
sketch of the argument. "Canto I.," he
says, "attempts to paint the ill effects of
over-joy; Canto II. those of excessive
melancholy. Part of the latter object
remains to be worked out in Canto III.,
which would likewise show that content-
ment with the mingled cup of humanity is
the true Nepenthe."

The third Canto unfortunately was never
printed, probably never written. The poem
remains a fragment, incomplete it is true,
yet of so majestic an outline, and so fully
instinct with the true spirit of romance, that
it seems hardly necessary to apologize for
this attempt to rescue it from the dust and
ruin of the past.

NEPENTHE

CANTO I

OVER a bloomy land untrod
  By heavier foot than bird or bee
Lays on the grassy-bosomed sod,
  I passed one day in reverie.
High on his unpavilioned throne
The heaven's hot tyrant sat alone,
And like the fabled king of old
Was turning all he touched to gold.
The glittering fountains seemed to pour
Steep downward rills of molten ore,
Glassily tinkling smooth between
Broom-shaded banks of golden green,
And o'er the yellow pasture straying
Dallying still yet undelaying,
In hasty trips from side to side
Footing adown their steepy slide
Headlong, impetuously playing
With the flowery border pied,
That edged the rocky mountain stair,
They pattered down incessant there,

B

To lowlands sweet and calm and wide.
With golden lip and glistening bell
Burned every bee-cup on the fell,
Whate'er its native unsunned hue,
Snow-white or crimson or cold blue;
Even the black lustres of the sloe
Glanced as they sided to the glow;
And furze in russet frock arrayed
With saffron knots, like shepherd maid,
Broadly tricked out her rough brocade.
The singed mosses curling here,
A golden fleece too short to shear!
Crumbled to sparkling dust beneath
My light step on that sunny heath.
Light, for the ardour of the clime
Made rare my spirit, that sublime
Bore me as buoyant as young Time
Over the green Earth's grassy prime,
Ere his slouch'd wing caught up her slime;
And sprang I not from clay and crime,
Had from those humming beds of thyme
Lifted me near the starry chime
To learn an empyrean rhyme.

No melody beneath the moon
Sweeter than this deep runnel tune!
Here on the greensward grown hot gray,
Crisp as the unshorn desert hay,
Where his moist pipe the dulcet rill
For humorous grasshopper doth fill,
That spits himself from blade to blade
By long o'er-rest uneasy made,

Here, ere the stream by fountain pushes
Lose himself brightly in the rushes
With butterfly path among the bushes,
I'll lay me, on these mosses brown,
Murmuring beside his murmurs down,
And from the liquid tale he tells
Glean out some broken syllables,
Or close mine eyes in dreamy swoon,
As by hoarse-winding deep Gihoon
Soothes with the hum his idle pain
The melancholy Tartar swain,
Sole mark on that huge-meadowed plain !

Hie on to great Ocean ! hie on ! hie on !
Fleet as water can gallop, hie on ! .
   Hear ye not thro' the ground
   How the sea-trumpets sound
Round the sea-monarch's shallop, hie on !

Hie on to brave Ocean ! hie on ! hie on !
From the sleek mountain levels, hie on !
   Hear ye not in the boom
   Of the water-bell's womb
Pleasant whoop to sea-revels, hie on !

Hie on to bright Ocean ! hie on ! hie on !
'Tis the store of rich waters, hie on !
   Hear ye not the rough sands
   Rolling gold on the strands
For poor Earth's sons and daughters, hie on !

Hie on to calm Ocean ! hie on ! hie on !
Summer-rest from earth riot, hie on !
   Hear ye not the smooth tide
   With deep murmur and wide
Call ye down to its quiet, hie on !

Thus to the babbling streamlet elves
To haste them down the slopes and shelves,
Methought some Naiad of their fall
In her bright-dropping sparry hall
Sang to her glassy virginal.—
   Perchance to me monition sweet !
I started upright to my feet
Attent : 'twas but a fancy dream !
I only heard in measure meet
 The pulses of the fountain beat,
As onward prest the throbbing stream.
Fair fall no less my fancy dream !
I have been still led like a child
My heedless, wayward path and wild
Thro' this rough world by feebler clues,
So they were bright, than rainbow dews
Spun by the insect gossamer
To climb with thro' the ropy air.
Fair fall ye then, my fancy dream !
I'll with this labyrinthian stream,
Where'er it flow, where'er it cease,
There be my pathway and my peace !

   Swift as a star falls thro' the night,
Swift as a sunshot dart of light,

Down from the hill's heaven-touching height
The streamlet vanished from my sight!

I crept me to a promontory
Where it had fallen from earth's top story,
And peering over, saw its flow,
A cataract white of smoke and snow,
Looping in fleecy shawls below;
Frail footing on such shrouds as these!
Elves may descend them if they please;
But here, by help of bushy stem
That plumes the hill's huge diadem,
By hoar rock, its gigantic gem
Far glancing o'er the prostrate seas,
Into the vale that spreads to them
Lark-like I'll drop by glad degrees.

Shrill on those lofty-sloping leas
The wind-bells sounded in the breeze,
Dingling beside me, as I glid,
So sweet, I scarce knew what I did;
But shrilly, too, as that lithe shell
Blown from old Ocean's world-broad well,
When the red hour of morn's begun
And Zephyr posts before the Sun.
Yet shriller still than rings at morn
The wet-mouthed wind-god's broadening horn,
Sudden above my head I heard
The cliff-scream of the thunder-bird,
The rushing of his forest wings,
A hurricane when he swoops or springs,
And saw upon the darkening glade
Cloud-broad his sun-eclipsing shade.

With the shrill clang that cleft the skies
When he flew Joveward with his prize,
The golden-haired Dardanian boy,
With such rude burst of robber joy,
Rose the sun-scorner; from earth's shore
My boy-weight like a worm he bore
Methought to heaven's embowed floor;
My brain turned—I could see no more!

O blest unfabled Incense Tree,
That burns in glorious Araby,
With red scent chalicing the air,
Till earth-life grow Elysian there!

Half buried to her flaming breast
In this bright tree, she makes her nest,
Hundred-sunned Phœnix! when she must
Crumble at length to hoary dust!

Her gorgeous death-bed! her rich pyre
Burnt up with aromatic fire!
Her urn, sight high from spoiler men!
Her birthplace when self-born again!

The mountainless green wilds among,
Here ends she her unechoing song!
With amber tears and odorous sighs
Mourned by the desert where she dies!

Laid like the young fawn mossily
In sun-green vales of Araby,

I woke, hard by the Phœnix tree
That with shadeless boughs flamed over me,
And upward called by a dumb cry
With moonbroad orbs of wonder, I
Beheld the immortal Bird on high
Glassing the great sun in her eye.
Stedfast she gazed upon his fire,
Still her destroyer and her sire !
As if to his her soul of flame
Had flown already, whence it came ;
Like those that sit and glare so still,
Intense with their death struggle, till
We touch, and curdle at their chill !—
But breathing yet while she doth burn
    The deathless Daughter of the sun !
Slowly to crimson embers turn
    The beauties of the brightsome one.
O'er the broad nest her silver wings
Shook down their wasteful glitterings ;
Her brinded neck high-arched in air
Like a small rainbow faded there ;
But brighter glowed her plumy crown
Mouldering to golden ashes down ;
With fume of sweet woods, to the skies,
Pure as a Saint's adoring sighs,
Warm as a prayer in Paradise,
Her life-breath rose in sacrifice !
The while with shrill triumphant tone
Sounding aloud, aloft, alone,
Ceaseless her joyful deathwail she
Sang to departing Araby !

Deep melancholy wonder drew
Tears from my heartspring at that view.
Like cresset shedding its last flare
Upon some wistful mariner,
The Bird, fast blending with the sky,
Turned on me her dead-gazing eye
Once—and as surge to shallow spray
Sank down to vapoury dust away !

O, fast her amber blood doth flow
 From the heart-wounded Incense Tree,
Fast as earth's deep-embosomed woe
 In silent rivulets to the sea !

Beauty may weep her fair first-born,
 Perchance in as resplendent tears,
Such golden dewdrops bow the corn
 When the stern sickleman appears.

But oh ! such perfume to a bower
 Never allured sweet-seeking bee,
As to sip fast that nectarous shower
 A thirstier minstrel drew in me !

My burning soul one drop did quaff—
Heaven reeled and gave a thunder-laugh !
Earth reeled, as if with pendulous swing
She rose each side through half her ring,
That I, head downward, twice uphurled,
Saw twice the deep blue underworld,
Twice, at one glance, beneath me lie
The bottomless, boundless, void sky !

Tho' inland far, me seemed around
Ocean came on with swallowing sound
Like moving mountains serried high!
Methought a thousand daystars burned
By their mere fury as they turned,
Bewildering heaven with too much bright,
Till day looked like a daylight night.
Brief chaos, only of the brain!
Heaven settled on its poles again,
And all stood still, but dizzily.

Light-trooping o'er the distant lea
A band I saw, where Revelry
Seemed on her bacchant foot to be,
And heard the dry tambour afar
Before her Corybantian car
Booming the rout to winy war.
Forward I felt my spirit chime
Awhoop with this hot-raging rhyme,
That, breathed up by the feverish crew
While back their Mænad locks they threw,
O'er them imbrowned the welkin blue.

Ambition mad, when most sublime!
Fain had I clomb Heaven's empery,
Fain would my Titan spirit climb
Mountain-topt mountain arduously,
To whoop the far uproar to me!
Such insane power and subtilty
The magic drop ethereal gave,
Tireless I clomb that palmy tree

And saw broad-landed Earth how brave !
Low on the horizontal lee
I saw, bedreamed, far ocean dumb
Upgathering his white skirts to come
Midland ; his arms twixt Araby
And Europe, Afric, India, spread
I saw ; the Mediterraneans three,
Azure, and orient grey, and red,
Washing at once the earth and sky ;
With the untravelled wastes that lie
Of greenest ocean, where the South
Swills it with demogorgon drouth,
Disgorging amid foam and roar
His salt draught back to every shore.

Mute as I gaze my feet below,
By times the silvery ashes glow
Under me, where the Bird of Fire
In her own flames seemed to expire,
Chanting her odorous monody ;
Methought in each faint glow, again
I saw her last dim glance at me
Languid with hope akin to pain.
" How, if the juice with ether rife,
Elixir of superfluous life,
Instinct with spiritual flame
Which from yon still of splendour came,
Might prove more quick restorative
Of her, than Hippocrat could give ! "

So thought I, and with fancy fired
Did what the draught itself inspired :

I sprinkled on the embers white
Few drops ; they curdle—close—unite,
Each with his orb of atomies,
Till in firm corporation these
Leaguing again by law occult,
Shapening and shapening by degrees,
Develop fair the full result ;
And like the sun in giant mould,
Cast of unnumbered stars, behold
The Phœnix with her crest of gold,
Her silver wings, her starry eyes,
The Phœnix from her ashes rise !

Now was the wherefore easy scanned,
She bore me from my bloomy land,
Threw on me her last filmed look ;
Smouldering aidless in her nook
Years had departed ere she grew
By sun and starlight bird anew ;
But their full essence poured in flame,
Distilment sweet !   Nepenthe true !
(By nature panacée sure, and name !)
Poured on her dust-dismembered frame,
Phœnix at once to heaven she flew !

Over hills and uplands high
Hurry me, Nymphs !   O, hurry me !
Where green Earth from azure sky
Seems but one blue step to be ;
Where the sun his wheel of gold
Burnishes deeply in her mould,

And her shining walks uneven
Seem declivities of Heaven.
Come ! where high Olympus nods,
Groundsill to the hall of gods !
Let us through the breathless air
Soar insuperable, where
Audibly in mystic ring
The angel orbs are heard to sing ;
And from that bright vantage ground
Viewing nether heaven profound,
Mark the eagle near the sun
Scorching to gold his pinions dun ;
With fleecy birds of paradise
Upfloating to their native skies ;
Or hear the wild swans far below
Faintly whistle as they row
Their course on the transparent tide
That fills the hollow welkin wide !

Hurry me, Nymphs !   O, hurry me
Far above the grovelling sea,
Which, with blind weakness and base roar
Casting his white age on the shore,
Wallows along that slimy floor ;
With his widespread webbed hands
Seeking to climb the level sands,
But rejected still to rave
Alive in his uncovered grave.

Light-skirt dancers, blithe and boon
With high hosen and low shoon,

'Twixt sandal bordure and kirtle rim
Showing one pure wave of limb,
And frequent to the cestus fine
Lavish beauty's undulous line,
Till like roses veiled in snow
Neath the gauze your blushes glow ;
Nymphs, with tresses which the wind
Sleekly tosses to its mind,
More deliriously dishevelled
Than when the Naxian widow revelled
With her flush bridegroom on the ooze,
Hurry me, Sisters ! where ye choose,
Up the meadowy mountains wild,
Aye by the broad sun oversmiled,
Up the rocky paths of gray
Shaded all my hawthorn way,
Past the very turban crown
Feathered with pine and aspen spray,
Darkening like a soldan's down
O'er the mute stoopers to his sway,
Meek willows, daisies, brambles brown,
Grasses and reeds in green array,
Sighing what he in storm doth say—
Hurry me, hurry me, Nymphs, away !

Here on the mountain's sunburnt side
Trip we round our steepy slide,
With tinsel moss, dry-woven pall,
Minist'ring many a frolic fall ;
Now, sweet Nymphs, with ankle trim
Foot we around this fountain brim,
Where even the delicate lilies show

Trangressing bosoms in bright row
(More lustrous-sweet than yours, I trow !)
Above their deep green boddices.
Shall you be charier still than these ?
Garments are only good to inspire
Warmer, wantoner desire ;
For those beauties make more riot
In our hearts, themselves at quiet
Under veils and vapoury lawns
Thro' which their moon-cold lustre dawns,
And might perchance if full revealed
Seem less wondrous than concealed,
Greater defeat of Virtue made
When Love shoots from an ambuscade,
Than with naked front and fair.
Who the loose Grace in flowing hair
Hath ever sought with so much care,
As the crape-enshrouded nun
Scarce warmed by touches of the sun ?
Nathless, whatsoe'er your tire,
Hurry me, sweet Nymphs, higher, higher !
Till the broad seas shrink to streams,
Or, beneath my lofty eye,
Ocean a broken mirror seems,
Whose fragments 'tween the lands do lie,
Glancing me from its hollow sky
Till my cheated vision deems
My place in heaven twice as high !

Ho ! Evoe ! I have found
True Nepenthe, balm of pain,
Sought by sagest wits profound,

Mystic Panacée! in vain.
Virtuous Elixir, this
Sure the supreme sense of bliss!
Feeling my impetuous soul
Ravish me swifter than Earth's roll
Tow'rds bright day's Eoan goal;
Or if West I chose to run,
Would sweep me thither before the sun,
Raising me on ethereal wing
Lighter than the lark can spring
When drunk with dewlight which the Morn
Pours from her translucent horn
To steep his sweet throat in the corn.
Still, O still my step sublime
Footless air would higher climb,
Like the Chaldee Hunter bold,
Builder of towery Babel old!
O what sweeter, finer pleasure
Than this wild, unruly measure,
Reeling hither, thither, so
Higher to the heavens we go!
Nymph and swain, with rosy hand,
Wreathed together in a band,
Like embracing vines that loop
Browner elms with tendril hoop,
Let us, liker still to these
In rich autumn's purple weather,
Mix, as the vineyard in the breeze,
Our wine-dropping brows together!
Swinging on our feet around
Till our tresses touch the ground,
That mad moment we do stay

To meditate our whirl-away !
Winds that, blown off the honied heath,
Warm the deep reeds with mellowing breath,
Shall for us, Æolian still,
These green flutes of Nature fill ;
On bluebell beds like dulcimers
Tingle us most fantastic airs ;
And where'er her numerous strings
Woodbine like a wind-harp swings,
Play us light fugues with nimble wings,
Trumpeting thro' each twisted shell
Till its mossy wrinkles swell.
Such shall, with sweet voluntaries,
Blithe accompaniment bear us,
Not without help of that dim band,
Minstrels of each woody land,
Piping unhired on every hand ;
These shall be our volatile chorus,
Fleeting the wilderness before us,
Like their small brethren of the chant,
Drone-winders itinerant,
Old-world humming birds, the bees,
Our sweet whifflers shall be these !
While our oval close within
Capering faun keeps mellow din,
With pipe and ceaseless cittern thrum,
Tinkling tabor's shallow drum,
Cymbal and lengthening cornmuse hum.
Uproar sweet ! as when he crost,
Omnipotent Bacchus, with his host,
To farthest Ind ; and for his van
Satyrs and other sons of Pan,

With swoln eye-burying cheeks of tan,
Who trolled him round which way he ran
His spotted yoke through Hindostan,
And with most victorious scorn
The mild foes of wine to warn,
Blew his dithyrambic horn !
That each river to his source
Trembled—and sunk beneath his course,
Where, 'tis said of many, they
Mourn undiscovered to this day.

Still my thoughts, mine eyes aspire !
Hurry me, sweet Nymphs, higher and higher !
Smooth green hills my soul do tire ;
Let us leave this lowly shire,
Tho' it be the Happy Clime,
'Tis for spirits less sublime !
Fleet we sheer as lightning-blast
Pinnacled Petrea past,
Burning rocks bestrown with sands !
O'er the bleak Deserta lands
Pass we, as o'er dead Nature's tomb,
Where Sirocco and Simoom
Battle with hot breath for room,
Tho' not even a flower or cress
Make war-worth that wilderness ;
From this wavering blown arene
To where the Rome-repelling queen,
High-stomach'd, star-bound Emperess !
Long beruled broad Palmyrene,
Let's begone ; and farther still,

C

Here, too, naught but sandblown hill,
Only another ocean bed
Tossed by billowy winds instead
Of the old legitimate breakers,
Dust-disturbers, not earth-shakers !
From these deep abysses dry,
Filled with sunlight to the sky,
Let us, O let us swift begone
To the cedared Lebanon ;
Over Carmel's flowery sides
Where the wild-bee ever bides,
Round each beauty of the glade
Singing his noontide serenade,
Till the ear-enchanted fair,
Opening her leafy stomacher,
Lets in the little ravisher. ·
On to shadowy Taurus, on !
Looming o'er the Syrian wave,
Scarce a flower his sides upon,
Swoln with many an antique grave
Of slaughtered Persepolitan,
Rare Greek and Macedonian.
Lowly shelter for the slain
Still his rueful heaths remain,
That purpler tinged with buried blood
Darken deeper the green flood,
And, a blushing chronicle,
The tale of fallen glory tell,
Persia's dumb echoes know so well !

Thou whose thrilling hand in mine
　Makes it tremble as unbid,

Whose dove-drooping eyes divine
 Curtain Love beneath their lid ;
Fairest Anthea ! thou whose grace
 Leads me enchantedly along
Till the sweet windings that we trace
 Seem like the image of a song !
Blithest Anthea ! thou I ween
Of this jocund choir the queen,
From thy beauty still more rare,
And a more earth-spurning air,
If forsooth my reeling vision
Hold thee steadily, and this
Be not my mind's insane misprision,
Drunk with the essence-drop of bliss !
Small matter !—while the dream be bright !
Surely thou with form so light
Must be some creature born for winging
Where the chimes of Heaven are ringing,
And sweet cherub faces singing
Requiems to ascending souls
Where each orb of glory rolls !
Bind me, oh bind me next thy heart,
So shall we to the skies depart,
And like a twin-star fixt in ether,
Burn with immortal flame together !

 That be our emprised rest,
Eyry where birds of Eden nest,
Warbling hymns in Wonder's ear !
We still walk this lowly sphere,
Lost in the heaven's crystalline mere
More than in ocean one small tear.

Wherefore, without vain delay,
Haste, Anthea! haste away
To those highest peaks the sun
Steps with glittering sandal on,
That this bosom-fire as fast
As his, breathe forth in the clear vast!

Bright-haired Spirit! Golden Brow!
Onward to far Ida now!
Leaving these garden lands below
In sea-born dews to steep their glow:
Caria and Lycia, dulcet climes!
Beds of flowers whose odour limes
The o'erflying fast far bird, their thrall
Hovering entranced till he fall;
Broad Mæonia's streamy vales
Winding beneath us, white with swans
Borne by their downy-swelling sails;
Each her lucid beauty scans,
Bending her slow beak round, and sees
Her grandeur as she floats along
Gracefully ruffled by the breeze,
And troats for joy, too proud for song.
Leave we the downlands, tho' be there
Joy a lifelong sojourner;
There for ever wildwood numbers
Poured in Doric strains dilute
T hro' the unlaborious flute,
othe Disquiet to his slumbers;
So his rosebed sleeps the bee,
In ed by Lydian melody,
Lull the honied morn in vain!
Half

Idler still the Doric swain,
Steeped in double sweetness he
Hums, as he dreams, his wildwood strain.
The Mysian vineplucker sings i' the tree,
And Ionia's echoing train
Of reapers, bending down the lea,
Make rich the winds with minstrelsy.

Here, no less, if any linger,
Pointing us down with abject finger,
Or stop with but a sigh to praise
The slothful fields on which we gaze
More time than serves him to renew
His buoyant draughts of ether blue,
Or (if the wine-sweat pouring through
With beaded reek his brows embrue)
Shake from his curls the shining dew—
Down with the grovelling caitiff, down !
Scourge him with your green thyrses down !
While as a thundercloud on high
Bursting its blackness o'er him, I
Envelop him in my blazing scorn
Of dread pride and bright anger born !
Here is meet repose for none
That climb Earth's mountain-studded zone !
Here the Great Mother smoothes again
Her broad skirts to the broader main !
Even Æolia's lofty steep
Shelves to the tributary deep,
And her level winds do play
His watery organ far away
To the hoarse Thermaic strand ;

Sleek as the tremulous lady moon
From her bright horizon chair,
Tipping his silver keys in tune
With long low arm and beamy hand
She stretches all enjewelled there.
Ida !—illoo ! behold ! behold
Ida, the Queen of the Hills of old,
Rising with sundropt crown of gold !
Alone great Ida from the shore
Lifts high above its silent roar
Her caverns, and with those rude ears
Only the haughty thunder hears !
All hail, green-mantled Ida !
Floodgate of heaven-fall'n streams !
Replenisher of wasteful ocean's store !
Sweetener of his salt effluence ! Ever-pure !
Battener of meagre Earth ! Bestower
Of their moist breath to vegetable things
That suck their life from thee !—
All hail !—
All hail, green Ida !—
Woody-belted Ida !—
Nurse of the bounding lion ! his green lair,
Whence he doth shake afar
The shepherdry with his roar ! All hail,
Peaks where the wild ass flings
His Pegasean heels against mankind,
And the more riotous mares,
Pawing at heaven, snuff the womb-swelling
      wind !
Ida, all hail ! all hail !
Nature's green, ever-during pyramid

Heaped o'er the behemoth brute-royal bones
Of monstrous Anakim !
All hail, great Ida ! throne
Of that old Jove the olden poet sung
Where, from the Gods alone,
He listened to the moan
Of his divine Sarpedon, thousand moans
    among !—
Ida, all hail ! all hail !
Thus on thy pinnacle,
With springy foot like the wild swan that
    soars
Off to invisible shores,
I stand ! with blind Ambition's waxen wings
High o'er my head
Outspread,
Plucking me off the Earth to wheel aerial
    rings !
Lo ! as my vision glides
Adown these perilous flowery sides,
Green hanging-gardens only trod
By Nymph or Sylvan God,
And sees o'er what a gulf their eminent glory
    swells,
I tremble with delight,
Proud of my terrible plight,
And turn me to the hollow caves
Where the hoarse spirit of the Euxine
    raves.
The melancholy tale of that drown'd Youth
    he tells
To the fast fleeting waves,

For ever in vast murmurs, as he laves
With foam his sedgy locks loose-floating
   down the Dardanelles !

   Down the Dardanelles !
What Echo in musical sound repels
My words, like thunder tolled
From the high-toppling rocks
In loud redoublous shocks
Behold, great Sun, behold !

   Down the Dardanelles !
Behold the Thunderer where she rides !
   Behold her how she swells
Like floating clouds her canvas sides !
Raising with ponderous breast the tides
On both the shores, as down she rides,
   Down the Dardanelles !

   Down the Dardanelles !
Each Continent like a caitiff stands,
   As every broadside knells !
While with a voice that shakes the strands
She spreads her hundred-mouth'd commands,
Albion's loud law to both the lands,
   Down the Dardanelles !

   Down the Dardanelles !
Ye billowy hills before her bowne !
   Wind caverns ! your deep shells
Ring Ocean and Earth her old renown

Long as that sun from Ida's crown
Smoothes her broad road with splendour
    down,
  Down the Dardanelles !

  Anthea, ever dear,
I feel, I feel the sharp satyric ear
Thy draught Circean gave me, echoing clear
  With that far chime !
Capacious grown enough to hear
The music of the lower sphere,
Tho' fainter than the passing tread of stealthy-
    footed Time !

Be mute, ye summer airs around !
Let not a sigh disturb the sound
That like a shadow climbs the steepy ground
Up from blue Helle's dim profound !
Listen ! the roar
Creeps on the ear as on a little shore,
And by degrees
Swells like the rushing sound of many seas,
And now as loud upon the brain doth beat
As Helle's tide in thunderbursts broke foam-
    ing at my feet !

Hist ! ho !—the Spirit sings
While in the cradle of the surge he swings,
Or falling down its sheeted laps,
Speaks to it in thunder-claps
Terrifical, half-suffocated things !
For ever with his furious breath

Keeping a watery storm beneath
Where'er he sinks, that o'er him seethe
The frothy salt-sea surfaces
Dissolving with an icy hiss,
As if the marvellous flood did flow
Over a quenchless fire below !
Hist ! ho ! the Spirit sings !

In the caves of the deep—lost Youth ! lost
    Youth !—
O'er and o'er, fleeting billows ! fleeting bil-
    lows !—
Rung to his restless everlasting sleep
By the heavy death-bells of the deep,
Under the slimy-dropping sea-green willows,
    Poor Youth ! lost Youth !
  Laying his dolorous head, forsooth,
  On Carian reefs uncouth—
    Poor Youth !—
On the wild sand's ever-shifting pillows !

In the foam's cold shroud—lost Youth ! lost
    Youth !—
And the lithe waterweed swathing round
    him !—
Mocked by the surges roaring o'er him
    loud,
" Will the sun-seeker freeze in his shroud,
Aye, where the deep-wheeling eddy has
    wound him ?"
    Lost Youth ! poor Youth !
  Vail him his Dædalian wings, in truth ?

Stretched there without all ruth—
      Poor Youth !—
Weeping fresh torrents into those that
    drowned him !

List no more the ominous din,
Let us plunge deep Helle in !
Thracia hollos !—what to us
Sky-dejected Icarus ?
Shall we less than those wild kine
That swam this shallow salt confine,
Venture to shew how mere a span
Keeps continental man from man ?
Welcome, gray Europe, native clime
Of clouds, and cliffs yet more sublime !
Gray Europe, on whose Alpine head
The Northwind makes his snowy bed,
And fostered in that savage form
Lies down a blast and wakes a storm !
Up ! up ! to shrouded Rhodope
That seems in the white waste to be
An icerock in a foaming sea !

This inward rage, this eating flame,
Turns into fiery dust my frame ;
Thro' my red nostril and my teeth
In sulphury fumes I seem to breathe
My dragon soul, and fain would quench
This drouth in some o'erwhelming drench !
Up ! to the frostbound waterfalls,
That hang in waves the mountain walls,
Down tumbling ever and anon

With long-pent thunders loosed in one,
Thro' the deep valleys where of yore
The Deluge his wide channels wore.
Hark ! thro' each green and gateless door,
Valley to echoing valley calls
Me, steep up, higher to the sun !
Hark ! while we stand in mute astound,
Cloud-battled high Pangæus hoar
With earthquake voice and ocean roar
Keeps the pale region trembling round !
Upward ! each loftier height we gain,
I spurn it like the basest plain
Trod by the fallen in hell's profound !
Illoo, great Hæmus ! Hæmus old,
Half earth into his girdle rolled,
Swells against heaven !—Up ! up ! the stars
Wheel near his goal their glittering cars ;
Ambition's mounting-step sublime
To vault beyond the sphere of Time
Into Eternity's bright clime !
Where this fierce joy
I feel, shall aye subside,
Like a swoln bubble on the ocean tide,
Into the River of Bliss, Elysium-wide ;
And all annoy
Lie drowned with it for ever there,
And never-ebbing Life's soft stream with
        confluent wave
My floating spirit bear
Among those calm Beatitudes and fair,
That lave
Their angel forms, with pure luxuriance free,

In thy rich ooze and amber-molten sea,
Slow-flooding to the one deep choral stave—
Eterne Tranquillity!
All-blessing, blest, eterne Tranquillity!

Strymon, heaven-descended stream!
Valley along, thy silver sand
Broader and broader yet doth gleam,
Spreading into ocean's strand,
Over whose white verge the storm
With his wide-swaying loomy arm
Weaves his mournful tapestry,
Slowly let down from sky to sea.
Strymon! up thy craggy banks
Mid the pinewood's wavering ranks,
What terrible howl ascends? What blaze
Of torches blackening the coil'd haze
With grim contrast of smoky rays?
What hideous features mid the flare,
Lit with yellow laughter? Where,
Ah! where my boon Circean band
Quiring round me hand in hand?—
Furies, avaunt! that dismal joy
Breeds me horrible annoy!
Avaunt, she-wolves! with rabid yell
Riving the very seams of hell
To swallow me and your rout as well!
Flee, flee, my wretched soul, from these
Erinnys and Eumenides,
Bacchants no more, but raging brood
Of fiends to feast them on hot blood!—
Down! down! and shelter me in the flood!

" Hollo after !—to living shreds tear him !—
    hollo after !
To the ravenous wild winds share him !—
    hollo after !
    Our rite he spurns,
    From our love he turns,
Hurl him the glassy crags down ! hollo after !
    With your torches blast him,
    To the broken waves cast him,
    Head and trunk far asunder !
    With a bellow like thunder,
Hollo after ! hollo after ! hollo after !"

Dull in the Drowner's ear
Bubbled amid far ocean these sad echoes drear.

In the caves of the deep—Hollo ! hollo !—
Lost Youth !—o'er and o'er fleeting billows !
Hollo ! hollo !—without all ruth !—
In the foam's cold shroud !—Hollo ! hollo !
To his everlasting sleep !—Lost Youth !

Canto II

Antiquity, thou Titan-born!
That rear'st thee, in stupendous scorn
At all succession. from thy bed
On prime earth's firm foundations spread,
And look'st with dim but settled eye
O'er thy deep lap, within whose span
Layer upon layer sepulchred lie
Whole generations of frail man!
That steady glare not fierce Simoom,
Blasting with his hot pinion blinds,
Nor floods of dust thy corse entomb,
Heaped o'er thee by the sexton winds!
Nor temple, tower, nor ponderous town
Built on thy grave can keep thee down,
But still thou rear'st thee in thy scorn,
Antiquity, thou Titan-born,
To crush our souls with that dim frown!
Strong Son of Chaos! who didst seem
Only a fairer form of him,
Moulding his mountainous profounds
To fanes and monumental grounds ;
His rocky coigns, with giant ease,
In pyramids and palaces
Piling aslope, as we with pain
His ruinous rubbish raised in vain!

Thou that with Tubal old compeer,
In living cliffs didst statue man
And carve, for toys, leviathan
Or mammoth, yet found bedded here
His stony limbs, where once he stood
Scarce moved a footpace by the Flood!
Still at thy works in mute amaze,
Sorrow and envy and awe we gaze!
Enlarge our little eyeballs still
To grasp in these degenerate days
Marvels that shewed a mighty will,
Huge power and hundred-handed skill,
That seek prostration and not praise
Too faint such lofty ears to fill!
From Ind to Egypt thou art one,
Pyramidal Memphis to Tanjore,
From Ipsambul to Babylon
Reddening the waste suburban o'er;
From sand-locked Thebes to old Ellore,
Her caverned roof on columns high
Pitched, like a Giant brood that bore
Headstrong the mountain to the sky:
That one same Power, enorm, sublime
Thou art, from antique clime to clime,
Eternal stumbling-block of Time!
Whose fragmentary limbs do stay,
Stones of offence, his difficult way,
And turn it o'er our works of clay.
Lo! where thy strength colossal lay
Dormant, within the deep-sunk halls
Of cities labyrinthian
Mid sandy Afric and the walls

Of sunburnt Syria or Deccan,
Up from the bilging globe he calls
Seas to surprise thee, or enthralls
Earth to deluginous ocean,
So far he may ; with foamy van
Whelming her shores where thou bedreamed
Heard'st not the tide that o'er thee teemed
Mountains of water ! Aye in vain !
O'ersailing vessels see below
Clear, thro' the glass-green undulous plain,
Like emerald cliffs unmoved glow
Thy towering forms stretched far a-main
By Coromandel, or that side
Neptunian Ganges rolls the tide
Of his swoln sire ; by Moab's lake
Whose purulent flood dry land doth slake
With bittern ooze, where that salt wife
Drinks her own tears she weeps as rife,
Empillared there, as when she turned
Back tow'rds her liquorish late-spent life
Where Shame's sulphureous cities burned :
By Dorian Sicily and Misene,
Upon whose strand thou oft didst lean
Thy temple-crowned head ; and where
Antium with opposite Carthage were ;
By green Juvernia's giant road
Paved from her headland slope and broad
Sands down to Rachlin's columned isle,
And dim Finn Gael's huge-antred pile
Where his vast orgue, high fluted, stands
Basaltic, swept with billowy hands
Oft, till the mystic chancel mourn

To weltering biers around it borne
Hoarse ritual o'er the wrecked forlorn ;
There did the scythed Demon hew
Sheer the Cyclopian causeway through,
Letting the steep Icelandic sea
In on the Ibernian and on Thee !
So from their icy moorings he,
Lopt cable, loosed the Arctic isles
Full sail, with mountainous weigh and prore
To force that boom of seadriven piles,
Bulwark against the Northern bore
Of Ocean, laid by thee, and now
Chaining the Strait, as long before,
Tho' scattered on the Southern bow
Kamchatka's sparry waters o'er—
What need for thy great relics plough
Tartaria sands, or seek that scroll
Which the rapt Bonze can scarce unroll,
Thy chronicle, in pagodas dim,
Lengthening it wave and wave a-flow
Incessant, as from darkness' brim
Wells forth Cathaian Hoan-ho ?
What need thy famous works be told
I' the New World, older than the Old,
If sooth the Mexique annals say
With Eve's first born, Tradition gray,
And monuments more fixed than they—
Pyramids baked in Noah's sun,
Dials and monstrous Gods, far back
Out-dating Denderah's Zodiac,
Crocodilopolis and Karnak ;
With scrolls of pictured speech begun

Ere smoother hieroglyph could run,
Slight copy of that primeval one ?
What need the wondrous town untomb,
Palenque, aye too old for Fame
To tell her antediluvian name
Or fate ; perchance, at her own door,
Crept back into Creation's womb,
Tired of endurance, thro' the chasm
Oped in Earth's side with mighty spasm
When Orinook burst forth, and down
From Chimborazo's streamy crown
Rolled oceanic Maranon,
Contributing fresh seas to seas ;
Huge chasm ! with Andes' ponderous chain
Locked to Eternity again,
The gulf of All as well as these.
Passing thy pierless bridges swung
Gorge over, darkening every dell,
With keystone rocks colossal hung
Like Sin's broad way from heaven to hell,
Sloping aloft with cliffy sides,
Thro' the burnt air the porchway rides ;
Demoniac shapes, devices grim,
Trenching the storied panels dim,
And mystic signs, dark oracles
Of Destiny, and Hell's decrees !—
Alas ! what scalding sand-wind rolls
Me to the sulphury rack of souls
Fierce on, and scarfs my victim eyes
With careless wreaths for sacrifice ?
Thus weep I, whirlwind-rapt amain :
Save me ! O save, ye mighty Twain,

Arbiters here twixt Sin and Pain !
Tho' Angels still of Judgment, be
Angels of Mercy now to me !
Bend down your level looks, or raise
One iron finger from the knee,
So Cherubin Pities sing your praise !—
Thus to a Twain that reared their forms
Like promontories o'er the storms,
Methought, dread Umpires of my doom,
Sitting impalled within the gloom
As ebon Seraphim by Night's throne,
Low at their feet I made my moan.
They stirred not at my prayer; but dumb,
Sate like the symbols of the world to come,
Immutable, inscrutable !
            I lay
Drowned in my heart-blood, wept away
Fruitlessly at those feet, long time,
Like the dust-clung, outcast corse of Crime.

A sigh that seemed to come from heaven
By some aerial Sorrow given,
Weeping his sublunar state—a sigh—
One faint far sound, like a swan's cry
Heard thro' the daffodils ere it die,
O'ercame my senses ; a sweet wail
Soothing me with its violet gale
To gentlest mood.   I looked—and lo !
Sweet as Love's star a crest did glow
On that now visible head I deemed
One of my Arbiter's.   Fair it beamed
With soft dilation, mellowing still

The heav'n-fall'n gem its saffron fire,
Crowning the radiant front until
Godlike and glorified entire :
The while, as there essayed his skill
Light-handed Zephyr o'er a lyre
With the bright hair strung like golden
    wire,
Dulcetly did the sunbeams thrill
Within that coronal attire,
Hailing the dawn! And at such hail
Behold a-peak the Orient dale,
Morning, with light-blown silver veil,
Stands dewy-eyed, and matron-pale ;
Breathing in smiles and tears upon
This sacred head her blessings dear,
As erst she did, each daylight peer,
Sad for her monumental Son.
O unchanged world! 'Twas Memnon here
Sat gazing with a mournful cheer
Still at his mother! Still with smile
Fond as her own would fain beguile
Her sorrow! Still each matin rise
Welcomed her bright tears with his sighs!
Most strange! most true! for I anon
Heard the famed chant heard long agone
By storiers sage, ascend the skies
From his Æolian barbiton ;
Soft parleying like the voice of rills
With Echo in the distant hills,
But versing words more liquid clear
Than those could, to a thirstier ear.

Thus, with a breezy rise and fall, rang the
    Memnonian rhyme,
Like the sweet-mouthed bells of heaven, wild
    but in one same chime.

      Winds of the West, arise!
Hesperian balmiest airs, O waft back those
    sweet sighs
     To her that breathes them from her own
     pure skies,
     Dew-dropping, mixt with dawn's engold-
     ened dyes,
       O'er my unhappy eyes!
From primrose bed and willow bank, where
    your moss cradle lies,
O from your rushy bowers, to waft back her
    sweet sighs,
      Winds of the West, arise!

      Over the ocean blown,
Far-winnowing, let my soul be mingled with
    her own,
     By sighs responsive to each other known!
     Bird unto bird's loved breast has often flown
      From distant zone to zone;
Why must the Darling of the Morn lament
    him here alone?
Shall not his fleeting spirit be mingled with
    her own,
      Over the ocean blown?

From your aerial bourne
Look down, O Mother, and hear your hap-
    less Memnon mourn!
  Spectre of my gone self, by sorrow worn,
  Leave me not, Mother beloved! from your
    embraces torn,
      For ever here forlorn!
For ever, ever lonely here! of all life's glory
    shorn!
Look down, O Mother! behold your hapless
    Memnon mourn,
      From your aerial bourne!

  The sweet Voice swooned, deep-thrilling;
    then
  Raised its wild monody once more
  As the far murmuring of the main
  Heard in a sea-shell's fairy shore,
  Scarce sensible, made one with pain,
  Wind-lost and fitfuller than before;
  Yet still methought the mystic strain
  Burden like this bewildered bore.

    O could my Spirit wing
Hills over, where salt Ocean hath his fresh
    headspring
And snowy curls bedeck the Blue-haired
    King,
Up where sweet oral birds articulate sing
    Within the desert ring—
Their mighty shadows o'er broad Earth the
    Lunar Mountains fling,

Where the Sun's chariot bathes in Ocean's
        fresh headspring—
        O could my Spirit wing!

O could this Spirit, prisoned here
Like thine, Immortal Murmurer!
In hatefullest bounds and bonds of clay,
O could this Spirit of mine away
To those strange lands—" Away! away!"
Methought the breeze with soft command
Raised itself in a sigh to say
After me, whispering still " Away!"
Still by my side re-echoing bland
In fervorous secrecy—" Away!"   .
The desert breeze with pinion gray
Rustled along the leafless sand,
Warning me still—" Away! away!"

    Not less than magic breath had blown
Ashy ambition now to flame,
Within me ; but like veins in stone
Red grew the blood in my cold frame :
Tho' drained this life-spring to the lees
On lancing rocks—this body worn,
Weed-wrung, and saturate with seas
Gulped thro'—by their wild mercy borne
Half jellied hither, and well nigh
Piecemeal by those white coursers torn
That shook their manes of me, foam high,
Cast on their saviour backs forlorn—
Tho' thus my flesh, my spirit still
Is unsubdued! aspiring will

Buoys up my sinking power. 'Tis thine,
This quenchless spark! To thee this glow,
This rise from my sea-grave I owe,
Nepenthe! vital fire divine!
Yet ah! what boots, if cup of bliss
Have such a bitter dreg as this?
Fragile and faint must I still on
The arduous path that I have gone,
Or burn in my own sighs! Like thee,
A winged cap, O Mercury!
I wear, that lifts me still to heaven,
Tho' down to herd with mortals driven.

Now as swift as Sadness may
Let me to those hills away,
Where the shadows of the Moon
Reach broad earth at brightest noon,
Where the Sun's car glittering
Waits at Ocean's fresh headspring,
And sweet oral birds do sing
Wild catches in the desert ring,
Mocking the changeful-crested King!
That must be where Cybele rears
Her tow'red head above the spheres,
Awful to Gods! where Eden high,
With terraced stairs that climb the sky,
Long lost to mortal ken doth lie.
E'en let me thither sad and slow
As wayworn he from thence doth go,

Reptilous Nile!—As shades that pass
Silent and soft o'er fields of grass,
So let my trackless spectre glide
His solitary wave beside.

    Hundred-gated City! thou
With gryphoned arch and avenue
For denizen giants, serve they now
But to let one poor mortal thro'?
Wide those streaming gates of war
Ran once with many a conqueror,
Horseman and chariot, to the sound
Of the dry serpent blazoning round
Theban Sesostris' dreaded name.
Where is now the loud acclaim?
Where the trample and the roll,
Shaking staid Earth like a mole?
Sunk to a rushes sigh!—Farewell,
Thou bleached wilderness o'erblown
By treeless winds, unscythable
Sandbanks, with peeping rocks bestrown,
That for thy barrenness seem'st to be
The bed of some retreated sea!
City of Apis, shrine and throne,
Fare thee well! dispeopled sheer
Of thy mighty millions, here
Giant thing inhabits none,
But vast Desolation!

    Fare well thee!—and lowly too,
Ye rev'rend sites, colossal names,

Esné and Ombos and Edfou,
Echoing still your bygone fames
In such ponderous syllables,
Howsoe'er forgotten else.
Over white-cliffed Elephantine,
Thro' thy quarries red and gray,
Womb of sublimity, Syene
Onward still I take my way :
Where broad Nile with deafening hymn
Enters the land of Mizraim,
O'er sounding cliffs made musical
By his wave-choral waterfall ;
Athwart high Nubia's tawny shelves,
Down which ploughing deep he delves,
Long strider of the level sands,
Three cataraĉt steps to lower lands.
Scarce my fiery breath I cool
In thee, hill-hollowed Ipsambul,
Where primeval Troglodyte
Turned the torrid day to night.
Helmed high within the gloom,
Thy pillaring statues sit sublime,
Taking, each side, colossal room
On granite thrones no king might climb,
And keeping halled state till Doom,
Co-templar Deities with Time.
Or before thy porch profound
By the choked river's antique roll,
From their seats, dry fathoms drowned,
Peering mildly over ground,
Head-free, along the desert shoal,
If not with form discumbered whole,

Looking blank on, as they did see
Far o'er this little earthy knoll
Into thy depths, Infinity.

    Narrowing now my path begins
Toward the lofty Abyssins;
Now in silk-soft fleece below,
Shrunk to miniature sound and show,
Tumbos' cataract seems to flow
A visual roar, and that high steep
Jebel Arambo, a step deep.
Now while this keen air renews,
On my strength its aim pursues,
From that old sand-swallowed Isle
Meroe, doubled by the Nile,
Balking before whose watery bar
Vainly Simoom his dragon cheers,
That sandward home from Senaar
Back on his stormy rider rears;
Fierce recusant to daggle still
His dusty wings at that blind will!
So I too, in dragon scorn,
With red breath like the desert-born,
Bicker against the winds that press
Me from that broad wilderness,
Westward then, where Nile divides
In two varicolour tides,
Milky and sable, I shall rise
By that soft galaxy to the skies.

Thanks, Nepenthe fine, for this
Living apotheosis !
Hark ! above me I do hear
Heavenly joybells ringing clear,
And see their golden mouths, ding-dong,
Vibrate with a starry tongue.
Welcome ! welcome ! still they toll
Syllabled sweetly in knell-knoll,
While more deep, with undulous swell,
Chimes unseen the burden-bell,
Mellowing, in the mighty boom
Of his huge sonorous womb,
Their sweet clangour, like the din
Of streams lost in a roaring lynn.
Twilight now o'er lawn and dale
Draws her dew-enwoven veil,
Tender-bosomed flowers to keep
Unruffled in their balmy sleep ;
Her's from planet fair and star
Day's last blushing Hour doth steal,
Those bright rivals to reveal,
And the Queen Moon, their non-pareil,
Rolling between her noiseless car,
Where in heaven-wide race they reel
Light splintering from each glassy wheel.
Small birds now thro' leafy shed
Rustling haste to bower and bed,
And the Roc, slow winnowing, sails
Heavily homeward thro' the vales
Clanging betimes, while they do cheep,
The tremblers, and more inwood creep.
Then shall not I, in some thick sward

Rest me, like gazelle or pard,
Brinded hyæna or zebir barred ;
Now that even these supple rovers
Hie to caves and healthy covers,
There to sleep till huntress Morn
Rouse them again with her far horn !

Solitary wayfarer !
Minstrel winged of the green wild !
What dost thou delaying here,
Like a wood-bewildered child
Weeping to his far-flown troop,
Whoop ! and plaintive whoop ! and whoop ?
Now from rock and now from tree,
Bird ! methinks thou whoop'st to me,
Flitting before me upward still
With clear warble, as I've heard
Oft on my native Northern hill
No less wild and lone a bird,
Luring me with his sweet chee-chee
Up the mountain crags which he
Tript as lightly as a bee,
O'er steep pastures, far among
Thickets and briary lanes along,
Following still a fleeting song !
If such my errant nature, I
Vainly to curb or coop it try
Now that the sundrop thro' my frame
Kindles another soul of flame !
Whoop on, whoop on, thou canst not wing
Too fast or far, thou well-named thing,

Hoopoe, if of that tribe which sing
Articulate in the desert ring !

Striding the rough mountain mane
Of Earth, her forelock now I gain,
Whence I behold the lucid spheres
As thick as ocean dropt in tears
On the sapphire-paven ciel,
That close now to my head doth wheel.
Brighter the Moon, and brighter glows !
Broader and broader still she grows !
On that steepling pinnacle
With glance rocks silver-slated down,
Her radiant ball sits tangible,
Huge pearl of Afric's mountain crown !
Ponderous jewel of Earth's crest !
There, star-studded she doth rest,
Filling every vale and lea
From her lucid fountain free,
Bank high, as with a crystal sea.
Flooded bright each woodland moves
Crisp as the sounding coral groves,
And each emerald lane doth seem
Bed of a diamond-watered stream.
But lo ! what mighty shadows cast
Their lengths upon the glittering vast
Portentous, as with giant reach
Eclipse thro' fields of air did stretch
Printing the lunar hills upon
Earth's disk in darkest colours dun ?
Ha ! more true shall Fantasy,
Twin-brother profane to Prophecy,

Interpret yon bright written sign,
Blazoning the dome with sense divine.
Yon far luminary stands
Apparent on these peaked lands,
Meanful device and monogram
Of their veritable name—
The Mountains of the Moon ! long known
On Afric's groin enormous zone,
But trod by mortal me alone !
'Less Gomer here did set his shoon,
Crossing to southern Zanguebar,
And call'd them Jebel-el-Gomar,
Arabiqued, Mountains of the Moon :
Since that double word implies
This sense, and toward the Star they rise
Her semblable footstool in the skies.

Now that she sinks amid the hills
And vaporous gloom her region fills,
Tearful light each orb distils,
Faintly closing his small eye !
Wrapt in stole of sablest dye,
Death-heavy Darkness on his throne
Nods like a corse !   What Anguish draws
That sigh, to make Existence pause,
And the deep slumberers under stone
Turn in their wormy beds and groan ?
Yet, a more terrible moan !
Like the buried Titan's sob
Bursting Etna's rocky chains
It shakes huge Afric with a throb,
Her stout girdle scarce sustains.

Hark, another !—but like the sound
Of hell's breath bubbling up thro' pools pro-
    found,
Sent forth in cloudy wise !
And now that Dawn, with flickering plumage
    gray,
Brushes the thick-spun web of Night away,
Two pools in mist and murmur bubble before
    mine eyes !
Black-watered that : right o'er
Its cave, a bust of Mauritanian mood,
Thick-lipt and carved in negro curls, as rude
As the grim lake itself in wavy tresses wore :
This ripples in soft ringlets, and sleek folds
Of milky undulance, eastward oozing
The hill's green shoulders down, diffusing
His wealth of waters o'er the humble wolds :
Not like his dark Brother making
His chasmy way, by choice, nor taking
Precipitous steps into the Atlantic holds.
Over the smooth well-front was seen
Cut in a stony table of Syene,
A head, of that colossal leaven,
But with mild looks, and patient eyeballs
    graven,
Waiting for day !
   ' She rose, maternal Morn !
With her first golden smile greeting the
    brow
Memnonian, and with balmiest sighs
Breathing her soul of love into those sanguine
    eyes

That gazed with large affection on the skies !
And like the joy of a faint-swelling horn
Heard far aloof, notes of glad welcome now
Rose from the steep front of the Goddess-
    born.

    Charactered underneath upon the stone
I read these mystic words alone :
Memnon—the God of the Blue River—the
    King
Of the Endless Valley—whoever his spirit
Will free from earthly fetters, let him mingle
A cup of darkness here with one of light,
Fit opiate for Life's fever,
And so be blest, pouring it on his brain.

    Two cups I mingled, dark and light,
From that black fountain and this white,
Pouring the opiate deftly down
The Nile-God's cleft and hollow crown,
As I divined his will.   The air
Grew vocal for a moment there,
With out-flown shriek of joy ; and where
Welkin aloft the sunbird sings,
I heard a clap and rush of wings,
As if some earth-pent spirit freed
Rose to the realms of bliss indeed !
Memnon from that day, by the shore
Of Nile, sits murmurless evermore !

    Thy claybound spirit is free, and mine
Still in this barry skeleton pine ?

No !—and I quaffed from either well
The mingled cup of heaven and hell !

Darkness began to hood the sky,
Methought, once more, the day to die
On this bleak death-bed, but not I !
From the sharp East a blackening wind
Came with broad vans the hills behind,
In her cloud-hung pavilion
Rolling Death's sable sister on,
Portentous Night ! Within the fold
Of its dark valance I was rolled
Whirling, steep down, as in a pall
Down the great gulf's eternal fall.

No sun came forth again ; but gray
As the still rocks on which I lay
Bleaching at last, endured the day.
O'er me the hard sky, massy-paven,
Seemed to be dropping crags from heaven
To make Earth dust, and hurricanes
Let scatter on her their whistling manes.
So, with his ensigns wet, Monsoon
Swept o'er the Mountains of the Moon,
Dreadfully calling cloud on cloud
From the deep South, that in thick crowd,
Swoln with the summons, bellying ran
To burst their rude strength in the van,
Till mass o'er mass enormous hurled
Heavily toppling stood the world !

Such terror vain Ambition waits
Still on the high tops he would tread :

E—2

Stand fast, ye thunder-shaken gates,
Against the rain-flood, o'er my head
Beating like ocean on his bed !
O let me wing unshent again
To sweet Earth's lowest, lowliest plain ;
Then let the rushing deluge sweep
Her proudest pinnacles to the deep !

Desert paths of the dry streams !
Swifter than the torrent teems
Scourged by South winds, as I flee
Spread your gray sands firm for me !
Pendant cliffs with sheltering brow
Shade me from destruction now !
Rocky steps of giant stride
Descending Afric, down your side,
Your unhewn smoothness let me slide !
Air ! O air, with thickening breath
Stay me not in the gripe of Death !
Back by the blown locks who doth still
Pull me to his cruel will ;
Let me into thy sightless sea
Like the poor minnow from the shark,
From those fell jaws that gape for me,
Plunge into deepest abysses dark !

Welcome dusky, unsunned dells,
Roofed with savage trees o'erblown,
Caverns in whose dripping cells
Hermit Sadness sits alone !

Eldern forests, whispering dim
Secrets in your dread Sanhedrim,
And nodding fate on those below;
Fearless thro' such inquest grim,
Rustling your mossy beards I go,
Fathomless falls for wild Despair!
Gulfs intransible of deep air!
Gladly from yon tempest I
To your terrible shelter fly.
Welcome, rocky vaults and rude
Cave-continued for the flood
That rolls his serpent-strength between,
Hissing beside me tho' unseen,
Thro' his vast ambush subterrene;
Chasms with cragged teeth beset,
Swallow me deeper, deeper yet!
Lowliest path is least unsure,
Most sublime, most insecure!
Fond Earth, within her parent breast
Finds us, weak little ones, safe room,
And thither pain or care opprest,
Sooner or later as their doom
All creep for refuge and for rest.

Shadowy aisles of pillared trees
Now my errant fancy please,
Dim cathedral walks like these;
Nave by numerous transepts crost,
Each in his own long darkness lost,
Cloister and chancel, thick embossed
Their roofs with pendant foliage, thro'
Whose fretted branchwork richly pours

The sun, in golden order due,
His bright mosaic on the floors.

Spreading now the darksome bourne,
Into warm twilight I return,
Still by these umbrageous eaves
Sheltered ; and where the thinner leaves,
With verdant panes, too bright illume,
Glance and pass forward into gloom
Thro' the dim-green air I hear
Only the rush of waters near,
Or see their spray a moment gleam,
Watermotes in the passing beam.

By that visionary shore
Steep channel of continual roar,
Billowy duct of flowing thunder,
That wallows the rooted woodland under,
Wandering I, in dizzy wonder,
Tread the hollow crust that caves
The rueful Erebus of waves
Beneath me surging. Blind I roam
The wilderness. O gentle Eve !
Pale daughter of the Day, receive
My greeting glad !—All hail, thou dome
Of God's great Temple, lit so bright
With lamps of ever-living light,
Kept trim within those censers rare
By Virgins quiring to their care,
Voice-joined, tho' separate in far air.
Awful Night ! thy sombre plumes,
Shadowed athwart the moonlight pale,

Make this rock-bestudded vale
Gleam like an antique place of tombs,
With lustre cold that chills the gale.
Grateful now to fallen me
This deep tranquillity!
Here in folded silence fast
Shall I fix myself at last,
Till I grow by age as grey
As the rocks, and stiff as they,
Making ever here my own
Statue and monumental stone!

   Cliff, of smoothest front sublime,
Tablet for that old storier Time!
What huge aboriginal sons
Of Earth, beat down by vengeful waves,
Sleep beneath these obliterate stones
In unmeasurable graves?
What mystic word inscribed can show
His terrible might who sleeps below?—
Sinews resolved to wreaths of sand!
Seams of white dust his bony frame!
His place on Glory's scroll doth stand
Blank—or filled up with others' fame!
Yet was he one that Pelion-high
Clomb perchance the difficult sky
Pelion on Oeta and Ossa heaved
Till of sight and sense bereaved,
Storm or sun stricken as I!
Ay, and shall Adam's pigmy sperm
Think to reach that sacred sphere
Which, from high-battled hills infirm,

No Briarean arms came near ;
Or think that his small memory dear,
Writ in the sands, shall aye survive,
While the eternal headstones here
Keep no giant name alive ?
The sands of thy own life, Renown,
Run between two creations down,
Few centuries apart ! What need
Glorious thought, or word, or deed,
When all mortal grandeur must
Lie with oblivion in the dust ?

Then hie on to humble lands !
On, still onward let me roam,
O'er sea-broad Sahara sands,
By the cataract's grizzled foam,
Where live-bounding he doth come,
Headlong Niger ! down the rocks,
Swept with his dishevelled locks,
Sable turned to silver flocks,
Like dark rain to driven snow,
When the blasts hibernal blow !
Now my steps as mute proceed
By his solitary roll
Winding round each desert knoll
As a gay enamelled mead,
With its yellow-blossom reed
Single bright thing that doth breed
There ; and rushy tufts of grass
Only sighing as we pass :
This wide waste of air unstirred
By the voice of bee or bird,

Even the soaring eagle's scream
Far off, like music in a dream
Imaged to the ear, is heard.
Strange pleasure in such wild to wander
Following murmurless Meander,
That loses his own serpent folds
Oft within the sabulous wolds.
May not I, ere these be crost,
Grave of all things living, be lost,
Now that in this inky lake,
Dry Afric's mediterranean,
Unsailed sea, the Mountain Snake
Buries his sightless head again?
Yet whate'er my soul inspire,
Purple sweet instinct with fire,
Or that late delirious draught,
Which from lunar wells I quaffed,
Still I turn where sand and sky
Spread in blank boundlessness to mine eye.

Thou, night-shaded Fountain! pure
Essence of darkness, deep distilled,
'Tis thou that hast my soul, most sure,
With thy sad infusion filled!
Else wherefore love I thus to tread
O'er the dust of Nature dead,
Buried in her own ashes gray,
Without one offspring of her womb
To strew her even a leafy tomb?
Wherefore love I thus to stray,
Finding joy in the lone wild,
Like Desertion's only child,

That in the sunburnt, silent air
Builds his crumbling castles there
And builds and plays with his despair?

    Solitude as deep and wide,
Treeless and herbless, never trod
Gray Triton underneath the tide,
Wandering the tawny barrens broad.
All is dumb, and the dead sands
Lie in long warps on both hands,
Furrows incult or barely sown,
Like desecrate lands, with salt alone,
Seed of sterility!—O more fleet
Must be my Arimaspian feet
To 'scape this dragon of the air,
Winding me round with sulphury flare,
Than the wild ostrich as she glides
Sheer onward with unpanting sides!

    Lo! in the mute mid wilderness,
What wondrous creature, of no kind,
His burning lair doth largely press,
Gaze fixt, and feeding on the wind?
His fell is of the desert dye,
And tissue adust, dun-yellow and dry,
Compaſt of living sands; his eye
Black luminary, soft and mild,
With its dark lustre cools the wild.
From his stately forehead springs,
Piercing to heaven, a radiant horn!
Lo, the compeer of lion-kings,
The steed self-armed, the Unicorn!

Ever heard of, never seen,
With a main of sands between
Him and approach ; his lonely pride
To course his arid arena wide,
Free as the hurricane, or lie here,
Lord of his couch as his career !
Wherefore should this foot profane
His sanctuary, still domain ?
Let me turn, ere eye so bland
Perchance be fire-shot, like heaven's brand,
To wither my boldness ! Northward now,
Behind the white star on his brow
Glittering straight against the Sun,
Far athwart his lair I run.

What marvellous things I saw besides,
Wandering heaven's wide furnace thro',
With floor of burning sands, and sides
And glowing cope of glassy blue,
Ne'er could mortal tongue nor ear
Intelligibly tell or hear !
Enow to have seen and sung of those
Beauteous chimeras, called in scorn,
Single of species both, and born
Mid among mankind, that but knows
The Phœnix and the Unicorn
Ev'n now, as dim-seen thro' a horn !
Both symbols of proud solitude,
One of melancholy gladness,
One of most majestic sadness,
And therefore to such neighbourhood

I won, by sympathetic madness,
Where let no other steps intrude!

Across the desert's shrivelled scroll
I past, myself almost to sands
Crumbling, to make another knoll
Amidst the numberless of those lands.
Welcome! Before my bloodshot eyes,
Steed of the East, a camel stands,
Mourning his fallen lord that dies.
Now, as forth his spirit flies,
Ship of the Desert! bear me on,
O'er this wavy-bosomed lea,
That solid seemed and staid anon,
But now looks surging like a sea.—
On she bore me, as the blast
Whirling a leaf, to where in calm
A little fount poured dropping-fast
On dying Nature's heart its balm.
Deep we sucked the spongy moss,
And cropt for dates the sheltering palm,
Then with fleetest amble cross
Like desert, fed upon like alm.
That most vital beverage still,
Tho' near exhaust, preserved me till
Now the broad Barbaric shore
Spread its havens to my view,
And mine ear rung with ocean's roar,
And mine eye glistened with its blue!
Till I found me once again
By the ever-murmuring main,
Listening across the distant foam

My native church bells ring me home.
Alas! why leave I not this toil
Thro' stranger lands, for mine own soil?
Far from ambition's worthless coil,
From all this wide world's wearying moil,—
Why leave I not this busy broil,
For mine own clime, for mine own soil,
My calm, dear, humble, native soil!
There to lay me down at peace
In my own first nothingness?